Pauline Cheyrouze

My horizon

Streets full of people, all eyes on me

SNAP COLLECTIVE PUBLISHING

Pauline Cheyrouze est une photographe professionnelle entrepreneuse passionnée par son métier. Elle est avant tout une personne très souriante, drôle et à l'écoute des autres. En tant que photographe, curieuse et ambitieuse.

Enfant, elle rêvait de devenir danseuse classique professionnelle. Malheureusement, à la suite d'une grave blessure, elle est contrainte d'arrêter. Elle se tourne alors vers la photographie. C'est une révélation ! Elle va se plonger dans les manuels techniques de la photo et lancer sa propre entreprise. Elle ne ferme aucune porte et décide d'exercer tout type de photographie. Elle devient ainsi photographe autodidacte de mode, de portrait, de publicité, de mariage et d'événements particuliers.

Pauline Cheyrouze is a professional photographer and entrepreneur. Passionate about her work, she is a very smiling, funny person who listens to others. As a photographer, she is curious and ambitious.

As a child, she dreamed of becoming a professional ballet dancer. Unfortunately, following a serious injury, she was forced to stop. She then turned to photography. It was a revelation! She immersed herself in the technical manuals of photography and started her own business. She does not close any door and decides to practice all types of photography. She became a self-taught photographer for fashion, portraits, advertising, weddings and special events.

MY
horizon

eyes on me

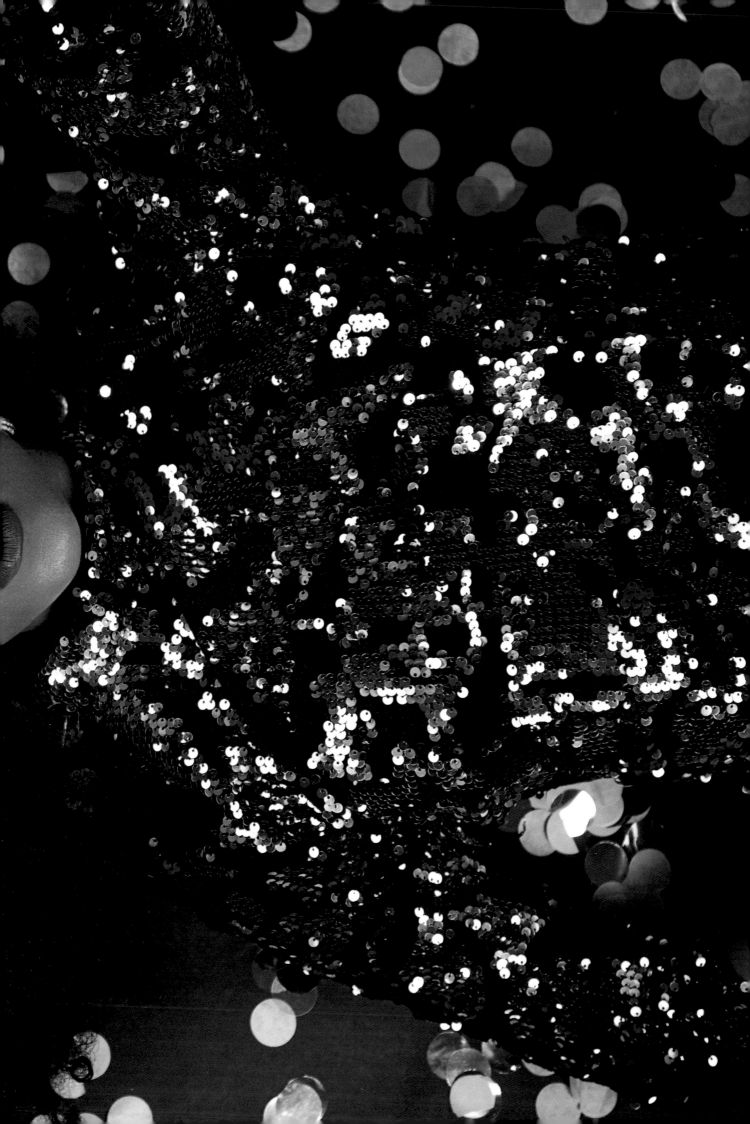

eyes on me

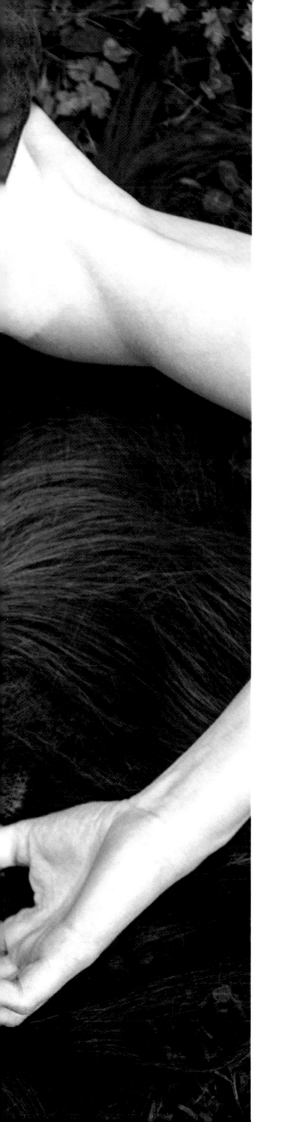

MODELS

Natalia, Clara Deswarte, Lucie Von Teese, Karina Katsan, Ola, Mylène Bude, Julia, Lisa, Olena, Natalia Verza (@mascarada.paris), Afrodite, Clémence Colombey, Elian, Calina Duca, Aurélie, Manon, Roman Fedorchenko

Imprint

Any brand names and product names mentioned in this book are subject to trademark, brand or patent protection and are trademarks or registered trademarks of their respective holders. The use of brand names, product names, common names, trade names, product descriptions etc. even without a particular marking in this work is no way to be construed to mean that such names may be regarded as unrestricted in respect of trademark and brand protection legislation and could thus be used by anyone.

Publisher:
Snap Collective
Is a trademark of
Rock N Books Ltd.
59 St. Martin's Lane, Suite 8, London, WC2N 4JS, UK

Printed at:
EsserDruck Solutions GmbH Untere Sonnenstraße 5, 84030 Ergolding

ISBN: 978-1-914569-30-2

Design by Olena Bidnenko
Editor Madara Ulme